Willow
the Wednesday
Fairy

For Evie Newberry,
with lots of love

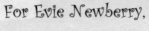

Special thanks to
Narinder Dhami

ISBN-10: 0-545-06758-8
ISBN-13: 978-0-545-06758-4

Copyright © 2006 by Rainbow Magic Limited.

All rights reserved. Published by Scholastic Inc., 557 Broadway, New York, NY 10012, by arrangement with Rainbow Magic Limited.

12 11 10 9 8 7 6 5 4 3   9 10 11 12 13/0

Printed in the U.S.A.

First Scholastic printing, August 2008

Willow
the Wednesday Fairy

by Daisy Meadows

SCHOLASTIC INC.

New York   Toronto   London   Auckland   Sydney
Mexico City   New Delhi   Hong Kong   Buenos Aires

The Fairyland Palace

Time Tower

Windy Lake

Tippington Town

Morristown Aquarium

The Tall Toy Store

Fashion Fun

Fountain

Dancing Days

Town Hall

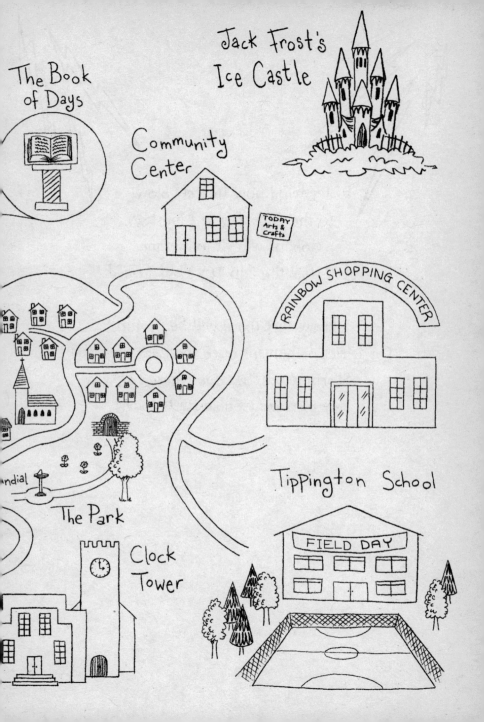

Icy wind now fiercely blow!
To the Time Tower I must go.
Goblins will all follow me
And steal the Fun Day Flags I need.

I know that there will be no fun,
For fairies or humans once the flags are gone.
Storm winds, take me where I say.
My plan for trouble starts today!

Contents

Arts and Crafts

"This is great!" Rachel Walker said, beaming at her best friend, Kirsty Tate, as they wandered around the Tippington Community Center Arts and Crafts Fair. "I don't know what to do first!"

The fair was in full swing. Wooden tables covered with long white cloths were arranged in a huge square, and

1

each table had been set up for different crafts. Rachel and Kirsty could see neat piles of velvet, satin, and silk fabrics for making patchwork quilts on one table, and knitting needles and baskets of fluffy wool on another. In one corner of the

square, a man was demonstrating origami, and in another Rachel's mom, Mrs. Walker, was teaching scrapbooking. Each table had space for people to try the crafts themselves, and there were already long lines at some of them.

"This *is* great, isn't it?" Kirsty said, looking around. "And I just thought of something. With so much colorful fabric and paper around, this would be the perfect place to find one of the fairies' Fun Day Flags!"

"You're right!" Rachel agreed. "Today is Wednesday, so we should be on the lookout for Willow's Wednesday flag."

Kirsty and Rachel shared a wonderful secret. They were friends with the fairies, and often helped them when icy Jack Frost and his goblins caused trouble. Now the girls were trying to find the seven magical flags that the Fun Day Fairies used to recharge their magic. That way, every day of the week would be filled with fun!

Jack Frost and his goblins had stolen
the flags, but the Fun Day magic had
made the goblins even more mischievous
than usual. Furious at the goblins' antics,
Jack Frost cast a spell to send the flags
to the human world. But the goblins
missed the fun so much, they snuck away
to try and get the flags back. Now the
fairies were relying on Rachel and Kirsty
to help them find the flags . . . before the
goblins did.

"I hope we can find
all the Fun Day Flags
before I have to go
home at the end of
the school break,"
Kirsty said. Then she
noticed that Rachel

was frowning. "What's the matter?" she asked.

"Have you noticed that no one looks very excited?" Rachel whispered, pointing at the visitors filling the room.

Kirsty looked around. Rachel was right. Even though some people were smiling, nobody looked like they were really having fun. "That's because Willow's Wednesday Flag is missing." Kirsty sighed.

Rachel nodded. "And it's going to be hard to find the flag with so many people around," she pointed out.

"Remember what the Fairy Queen always says," Kirsty reminded her. "We have to let the magic come to us."

Rachel smiled. "You're right," she said. "Which craft should we try first?"

"Look, there's no line at the jewelry-making table," Kirsty pointed out. "Let's start there."

The girls hurried over. The table was covered with bracelets, necklaces, and earrings, all

made out of sparkling beads in different colors.

"Hello, girls," the jewelry maker said, smiling. "Would you like to make some bracelets?"

"We would love to!" Kirsty replied.

She and Rachel sat down and the man gave them each a pair of scissors, string, and a silver clasp.

"First, cut the string to fit your wrist," he explained, as he pulled out a large plastic box with lots of little drawers from under the table. "Then thread these beads onto your string to make your bracelet. You can use any of the beads you like."

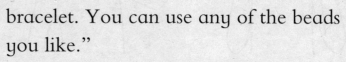

Rachel and Kirsty measured each other's wrist and cut their strings, as the man went to talk to someone at another table. Then, eagerly, they opened the tiny drawers.

"Ooh, these are pretty!" Rachel gasped, as they looked through different-sized beads in all the colors of the rainbow.

The girls began threading beads onto their bracelets. Rachel was using sparkly beads of all different sizes, while Kirsty had chosen tiny pink and purple ones.

Soon, Kirsty realized that the drawer of small pink beads was almost empty, and she still had the last part of her bracelet to finish. She began checking the other

drawers, hoping to find more pink beads somewhere.

Suddenly, Kirsty's heart skipped a beat. A faint glittery green sparkle was swirling around one of the drawers. Kirsty gently pulled the drawer open and peeked inside. A tiny fairy was smiling up at her!

"Rachel," Kirsty whispered happily, nudging her friend. "It's Willow the Wednesday Fairy!"

Bits and Pieces

Willow looked thrilled to see the girls.
She wore a flowing dress in different
shades of green, and had little green
slippers on her feet.

"Hello, Willow," Rachel said. "Have
you come because the Wednesday flag is
somewhere nearby?"

Willow peeked cautiously out of the

drawer. The jewelry maker was facing the other way, chatting to the woman at the potter's wheel. Willow leaped lightly out of the box and hovered in front of the girls.

"Yes, Rachel," she declared. "I think my flag is here. And the poem in the Book of Days will help us find it."

The Book of Days was kept by
Fairyland's Royal Time Guard, Francis
the frog. Every morning, Francis checked
which day it was in the Book of Days,
and then raised the correct Fun Day
Flag up the flagpole at the top of the
Time Tower. When the sun hit the
Fun Day Flag, the magical rays would
shine down into the courtyard, where a
fairy would be waiting to charge her
wand with Fun Day magic. Ever since
the flags had been stolen, poems had
magically appeared in the Book of
Days, giving clues about where each
flag might be.

"Tell us the poem, Willow," Kirsty
said eagerly.

Willow began to recite:

"Yards of fabric, strings of beads
Follow the glitter, see where it leads.
It once was one, but now it's three;
The Wednesday Flag means fun and glee!"

"It once was one, but now it's three," Rachel repeated. "What does that mean?"

"I don't know," Kirsty replied. "But I  think the first part means we have to follow a trail of glitter." Willow nodded. "But first, let me finish your bracelets for

you." She lifted her wand and a shower
of emerald sparkles floated down onto
the two bracelets. Immediately, more
beads magically
appeared on the
bracelets, and
the clasps
shut neatly
into place.

The
jewelry
maker was
coming back,
so Willow quickly
zoomed over to hide
in Rachel's pocket.
Meanwhile, the girls put their
bracelets on.

"Look," Willow whispered, leaning

out of Rachel's pocket and pointing at
the floor with her wand. "Glitter!"

Rachel and Kirsty looked down and
saw a small pile of gold glitter on the
floor near the jewelry table.

"It's not really a trail of glitter,
though," Kirsty said doubtfully. "It's just
a little pile."

"There's a button and some ribbon next to it," Willow pointed out.

"And another pile of glitter a little farther on," Rachel added.

The girls thanked the jewelry maker for their bracelets, then hurried over to the second pile of glitter. Now they could see that there was a scattered trail of glitter, buttons, ribbons, fabric, and beads.

"Where does it lead?" Willow whispered eagerly.

Rachel and Kirsty carefully followed the glitter trail. It led them right to the quilting table, where several people were sewing different pieces of brightly colored fabric onto a beautiful patchwork quilt.

At that moment, a woman put down her needle and reached for a new piece of fabric. Rachel and Kirsty noticed that the fabric squares were stacked in neat piles on one side of the table.

On top of one pile was a beautiful piece of golden cloth with glittery patches.

Rachel nudged Kirsty. "The pattern on that gold material looks just like the pattern on the Fun Day Flags," she murmured. "But it couldn't be Willow's flag, could it?"

"I don't think so," Kirsty said,

frowning. "It looks much smaller than the other flags we've found."

Willow peeked out of Rachel's pocket to look at the gold material. As soon as she saw it, a big smile lit up her face. "It *is* my flag!" she whispered. "Well, part of it, anyway. Remember that the poem

said, *'It once was one, but now it's three'*?
My flag must be in three pieces."

"Oh, no!" Kirsty exclaimed in horror.
"You mean the flag has been ruined?
What will we do now?"

Crafty Goblins

"Don't worry," Willow replied quickly.
"As long as we find all three pieces, I can
make the flag as good as new with my
fairy magic."

The three friends stared longingly at
the piece of flag lying with the other
fabrics. The woman running the table
saw them looking and smiled.

"That's a pretty fabric, isn't it?" she remarked.

Rachel nodded as an idea popped into her head. "Do you think I could have it for a project I'm doing?" she asked. "I'll pay for it."

"Of course you can have it, my dear," the woman replied. "I think we have some more pieces of that same cloth somewhere, too." She turned away and began hunting around the table.

Kirsty and Rachel glanced at each other in delight. Were they really going to get all three pieces of Willow's flag back all at once? But to the girls' disappointment, the woman returned empty-handed.

"I'm sorry," she said, frowning. "I had a large piece that I cut up earlier today. But I can't find the other pieces." She picked up the one piece of the flag and handed it to Rachel. "We haven't used any in the quilt yet, so I don't know where the other pieces have gone."

"Thank you," Rachel said gratefully, tucking the material safely into her pocket. Then she turned back to Kirsty, looking anxious. "Where are we going to look for the other pieces?" she asked quietly.

Kirsty was staring at the floor. "It's OK," she told Rachel. "The glitter trail keeps going. Look!"

"Oh, good!" Rachel said with a sigh of relief.

"Let's go!" Willow added.

The friends eagerly began following the sparkly glitter trail again. Along with the glitter, they saw broken crayons, beads, and embroidery string. This time, the trail led them to the origami table, where people were learning how to fold paper into colorful fish, flowers, and birds.

"Kirsty, the glitter trail goes under the tablecloth!" Rachel whispered.

"Do you think the trail continues under there?" Kirsty asked.

Rachel lifted a corner of the tablecloth to check. To her surprise, she saw four big green feet hurrying by. Goblins! Cautiously, she lifted the tablecloth a little further and peered at the two goblins. They were carrying huge piles of cloth, paper, and glue in their arms. Luckily, they were too busy muttering gleefully to each other to notice Rachel. The goblins hurried along under the row of

tables, completely hidden by the long
tablecloths.

"There are goblins under the tables!"
Rachel whispered. Kirsty's eyes opened
wide, and Willow, who was peeking out
of Rachel's pocket, gasped in surprise.

"I bet they're up to no good!" Kirsty said.

"They're probably looking for the Wednesday flag!" Willow added. "Maybe they have some of the missing pieces."

"We'd better follow them," suggested Kirsty. "But we'll have to be fairy-sized to do that."

Rachel glanced around. "There are too many people here," she said. "Someone might see us!"

"Look," Willow whispered, pointing her wand at a dressmaking booth. "There's a screen there for trying on clothes."

"Perfect!" Kirsty exclaimed. She and
Rachel hurried over and slipped behind
the screen when no one was looking.

Willow immediately flew out
of Rachel's pocket and
showered the girls
with sparkling fairy
dust. In the
twinkling
of an eye,
Rachel and
Kirsty were tiny
fairies with
shining wings.

"Now we must
fly low," Willow
warned, "and get
underneath the closest
table as fast as we can!"

The girls followed Willow as she
fluttered out from behind the screen, and
dodged the legs of people clustered at the
sewing table. Finally, they darted safely
under the tablecloth and out of sight.

"This way," Rachel said, pointing in
the direction the goblins had gone.

They flew along slowly underneath
the square of tables, careful to avoid the
boxes and bags that were stored there.

"I can hear giggling," Kirsty whispered.

Willow nodded. "That's a goblin giggle," she said confidently. She motioned to the girls and they flew behind a large plastic storage box. Then they all peeked out carefully from behind it.

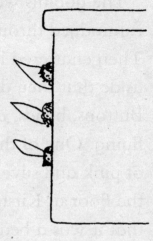

The goblins were sitting underneath the next table. They had collected all sorts of materials and were sticking them onto a big piece of cardboard. Willow and the girls could see buttons, beads, wool, pieces of fabric, and colorful paper scattered around them.

"The goblins are making a collage!" Willow murmured.

The goblins were having a blast as they rummaged through their craft supplies. They chattered happily and tossed things aside that they didn't want to use. Buttons, beads, and colored paper went flying. One of the goblins tossed a piece of pink and silver paper, which landed on the floor at Kirsty's feet. She could see that it was a beautiful butterfly from the origami table.

"Look!" Rachel gasped, her voice full of excitement. She was pointing at the goblin's pile of supplies. "I can see another piece of Willow's Wednesday flag!"

Butterfly Fun

Kirsty and Willow looked and saw the piece of sparkly gold material among the goblins' things.

"That's why the goblins are having so much fun!" Willow said.

Rachel frowned. "If they knew they had part of the flag, wouldn't they be taking better care of it?" she said thoughtfully.

"You're right!" Willow agreed.
"Which can only mean that the goblins
are so silly, they don't realize they have
part of my flag! Maybe we can get it
back before they notice."

"We need to lure the goblins away so
we can grab it," Kirsty said. She glanced
down at the origami butterfly at her feet.
"I have an idea!"

Quickly, Kirsty whispered her plan to
Willow. The fairy smiled and raised her
wand, sending a few sparkles of fairy
magic drifting down onto the delicate
paper butterfly.

Kirsty and
Rachel watched
as the butterfly
began to beat its
pink and silver
wings. Then
it fluttered
up into the
air and danced
gracefully toward
the goblins.

The first goblin
glanced up as
the butterfly came

41

closer. His eyes opened wide, and he nudged the other goblin in the ribs.

"Look, a butterfly!" he said. The second goblin looked up and noticed the butterfly, too. "Oh yes," he agreed. "Look at its shiny wings!" Losing interest in the collage, both goblins jumped to their feet and rushed after the butterfly as it flew by.

"Come on!" Willow whispered. The friends hurried over to the pile of beads and buttons. Willow waved her

wand above the piece of flag, and it
immediately shrank so that Rachel could
tuck it into her pocket.

"Now we have two pieces!" Rachel
said happily.

The goblins hadn't noticed the girls.
They were still too busy trying to catch
the butterfly.

"Where did you come from, butterfly?"
the first goblin asked, reaching for it.
This time he caught it, but as soon as he
touched it, Willow's magic disappeared
and the butterfly became a piece of
paper again.

Willow and the
girls couldn't
help laughing at
the confused
look on both
goblins' faces.

"You broke it!"
the second goblin
wailed, while the first goblin unfolded the
paper, scratching his head as he tried to
figure out what had made it fly.

"What now?" asked Kirsty.

"Look," Willow said, pointing at the
floor. "There's
more of the glitter
trail!"

The girls and
Willow flew on,
following the
trail. It led them
around a corner, and
suddenly, there were two more goblins
in front of them! They marched along
happily, chatting and chuckling. One of
them was holding the last piece of the
Wednesday flag in his hand!

A Lasting Impression

In a flash, the friends dove behind a large bag and peeked out to see what the goblins were up to.

"Well, we have one piece of the flag, but what about the rest of it?" the first goblin was saying.

"The others are too busy having fun to

look for the missing pieces," the second
goblin giggled.

"We'd better go and remind them,"
the first goblin said. Then he grinned.
"We'll sneak up behind them and shout,
BOO! That will scare them out of
their skins!"

"Oh, good idea," the second goblin
agreed, roaring with laughter.

"That piece of my flag means they're
full of fun!" Willow
whispered, as she
and the girls watched
the goblins heading off
to find their friends.
"We have to get that
last piece back!"

Rachel and Kirsty
thought hard.

Suddenly, Rachel's face lit up. "Maybe we can distract those two goblins by helping them have some more fun," she said. "I saw a big tub of clay underneath the sculpture table when we flew by. If we can get the goblins to try making hand impressions, they'll have to put the flag down."

"That's a great idea!" Willow exclaimed.

"We'll have to get back to the sculpture table fast, though," Kirsty pointed out. "The goblins are already ahead of us!"

"How are we going to pass them without being seen?" asked Rachel.

"We could slip out from underneath the tables," Willow suggested, "fly really fast along the outside, and then, once we've passed the goblins, dive under the

tables again. We'll just have to be careful
that nobody sees us."

Rachel and Kirsty nodded and
followed Willow out from under the
tablecloth. The little fairy shot off so fast
she was almost a blur. Rachel and Kirsty
zoomed after her,
dodging legs as
they wove their
way in and out
of the people
standing around
the tables.

Finally,
Willow swooped
underneath the
sculpture table,
followed closely

by the girls. The big tub of clay Rachel
had noticed earlier was still there. Kirsty
could hear the goblins approaching.

"We made it." Kirsty gasped. "Here
come the goblins!"

"Argue with me, Kirsty,"
Rachel said in a low
voice. "I want to
go first!" she
added loudly.

"No, me
first! Me first!"
Kirsty protested,
pretending to
glare at Rachel.

The goblins heard
them and looked over at the
girls curiously.

"It's very important to be first," Willow said. "Maybe it should be me."

"It was my idea. I'll go first," Rachel argued.

"No! Me first!" one of the goblins snapped, marching over and elbowing Rachel aside.

"No, me!" the goblin with the flag
yelled rudely, following his friend. Then
he stared at the clay, looking confused.
"What are you doing?"

"Putting our hands in the clay to make
impressions of them," Kirsty explained.

"Let's give it a try!" the first goblin said
to his friend.

But the second goblin
shook his head
firmly. "I can't,"
he muttered,
clutching the
piece of flag tightly.
"I have to hold this."

Kirsty and Rachel were
dismayed, but then Willow
joined in.

"Why don't you do your feet?"
she suggested. "That way,
you won't have to let go
of anything."

The goblin's face
brightened. "Oh
yes!" he agreed.

Both goblins
climbed eagerly onto
the edge of the tub.

"On the count of
three," Kirsty
called. "One,
two, THREE!"

The goblins
jumped into the clay
and landed with a splash, sinking down
into it. Immediately, Willow waved her

wand and fairy dust swirled around
the tub.

"Hey!" the first goblin
shouted, trying to pull one
of his feet out of the
clay. "I can't move!"

"The clay is set
hard!" roared the
second goblin
furiously, swaying
from side to side as
he tried to escape.
"You tricked us!"
Laughing, Rachel
and Kirsty flew
over and pulled the
piece of flag easily
from his hands.

Both goblins yelled and grumbled, but they couldn't do anything to stop the girls. Willow used her magic to shrink the flag fabric, and Rachel put it in her pocket with the other pieces.

"We have all three pieces of my Wednesday flag back at last!" Willow declared, her eyes shining with happiness. Their plan had worked perfectly!

Fairy Painting

"Let us go!" the goblins yelled angrily as Willow and the girls flew away.

"My spell will wear off in a few minutes," Willow told Rachel and Kirsty. "But that will give me just enough time to put my flag back together and take it home to Fairyland."

Once they were safely out of sight of

the goblins, they stopped. Rachel took
all the pieces of the flag out of her pocket,
and she and Kirsty laid
them carefully on the floor.
Then Willow waved
her wand. With a
flash of magic
sparkles in all
the colors of the
rainbow, the flag was whole again.

"You can't even tell that it was ever
cut up!" Rachel said, staring at the
beautiful flag.

Willow nodded happily. Then she
grinned. "I'll have to make you human
again while we're out of sight under
here, girls," she said. "Be careful not to
hit your heads."

With another wave of her wand,

Willow turned Rachel and
Kirsty back to their
normal size. The girls
crouched on their
knees, trying not to
bump into the table.

"Thank you, girls,"
Willow said. "I have
to go to Fairyland
now and recharge my
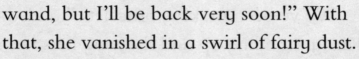
wand, but I'll be back very soon!" With
that, she vanished in a swirl of fairy dust.

Cautiously, Rachel and Kirsty crawled
out from under the table, hoping no one
would notice them.

"Girls!" Mrs. Walker exclaimed.

Rachel and Kirsty looked up to see
Rachel's mom standing staring down at
them in amazement.

"What are you doing under my table?"

Rachel and Kirsty grinned at each other. They hadn't realized they were underneath Rachel's mom's table!

"We were just helping clean up," Rachel said quickly, picking up some scissors she had noticed lying on the floor.

"We've been making bracelets," added Kirsty, standing up and showing hers to Rachel's mom.

"Oh, they're lovely!" Mrs. Walker exclaimed, examining it. Then she glanced at her watch. "You know, there's still an hour before the fair closes. Why don't you go try something else?"

"OK," said Rachel. "Come on, Kirsty!"

"What should we try next?" Kirsty asked as they wandered around the room.

"I've always wanted to try using a potter's wheel," Rachel said. "Or what about the embroidery table?"

"Both sound fun to me," Kirsty replied. "I just hope Willow was able to recharge her wand by now!"

"Psst!" came an urgent whisper.

Rachel and Kirsty stopped and looked around. Then, seeing a faint glow of fairy magic around one of the tablecloths, they bent down and lifted the corner. There was Willow, hovering under the embroidery table.

"Hello, girls!" She beamed. "Look!"
She waved her wand a couple of
times. Kirsty and Rachel
saw a stream of magical
sparkles flow underneath the
tables, swirling and zooming
from one to the other.
"I recharged my wand
with Fun Day magic. Wednesday will
be a lot more fun from now on!"
Willow promised.

Kirsty and Rachel glanced at each
other in delight.

"Everyone in Fairyland was thrilled,"
Willow went on. "The king and queen
and Francis told me to thank you for all
your help! Now, I have to get going,
but" — she winked at the girls — "you
might like to try model-painting before you

go home. Good-bye!" And with another swirl of fairy dust, Willow was gone.

"Model-painting?" Rachel said, glancing around the hall. "Where's that?"

"Over by the origami table," said Kirsty, pointing.

The girls hurried to the table, where people were sitting painting models of birds and animals.

"Hello, girls," the woman running the table said, smiling. "Would you like to join us? Here are some paints for you. I'll go and see what models we have left."

Rachel and Kirsty found two empty

seats. But the woman came back a few minutes later, looking puzzled.

"I don't even remember packing these," she said. "But I seem to have a lot, and I thought you might like them."

She put two beautiful fairy models down on the table. Rachel and Kirsty could hardly believe their eyes.

"It must have been Willow's magic!" Rachel whispered, and Kirsty nodded.

"Here's some wire to make wings," the woman went on.

People standing around the table were also starting to notice the pretty models.

"Mom, can I try?" asked one little girl.

"Me, too!" another one said eagerly.

Soon, the table was full of people

painting the delicate
fairy models and
fixing wire wings to
their backs.

Everyone chattered
happily as more and
more people crowded
around to join in.

"We're not the only people at the fair
who are having fun," Rachel said to
Kirsty, as they finished painting their
models in different shades of green to
look like Willow. "Look at all these
smiling faces!"

Kirsty grinned. "Yes, Willow's Fun
Day magic is working perfectly again,"
she agreed. "Let's hope we can make
tomorrow just as fun by finding
another flag!"

RAINBOW magic™

THE FUN DAY FAIRIES

Megan, Tara, and Willow all have
their magical flags back. Can Rachel
and Kirsty bring the sparkle back to
Thursday by helping

Thea
the Thursday
Fairy?

Spectactular Seahorses

"A tropical reef, a sunken ship, sea otters, seahorses, giant Japanese spider crabs, reef sharks . . . wow!" Rachel Walker looked up from the colorful brochure she was holding and grinned at her friend, Kirsty Tate. "We're going to have a fabulous time here!"

The two girls had come to the

Morristown Aquarium for the day with Rachel's parents. Kirsty was spending the week of school vacation with Rachel, and they had been having a very exciting time. A very magical time, too!

"We'll meet you back here at four o'clock," Mrs. Walker said, as they all strolled into the entrance lobby. "Have fun!"

"We will," Rachel said cheerfully, but then she gazed at some of the other people nearby. "Although it doesn't look as if anyone else is having much fun," she whispered to Kirsty.

Kirsty looked around. Rachel was right. There were plenty of visitors at the aquarium, but they didn't seem to be enjoying themselves.

"I don't even like fish," they heard one

boy mutter. "Why did we have to come here?"

Rachel and Kirsty gave each other a knowing look as Rachel's parents wandered off to look at the first exhibit. They knew exactly why the mood at the aquarium was so glum. It was because the Thursday Fun Day Flag was missing!

Kirsty turned to Rachel. "We've just got to find that Thursday flag before the goblins do," she whispered. "We really need to cheer everybody up in here."

Come flutter by Butterfly Meadow!

Butterfly Meadow #1: Dazzle's First Day
Dazzle is a new butterfly, fresh out of her cocoon. She doesn't know how to fly, and she's all alone! But Butterfly Meadow could be just what Dazzle is looking for.

Butterfly Meadow #2: Twinkle Dives In
Twinkle is feisty, fun, and always up for an adventure. But the nearby pond holds much more excitement than she expected!